Baby Bi

Kathy Storms
illustrations by James Storms

ISBN: Softcover   978-1-7960-3708-1
        Hardcover   978-1-7960-3709-8
        EBook   978-1-7960-3707-4

Print information available on the last page

Rev. date: 06/04/2019

To order additional copies of this book, contact:
Xlibris
1-888-795-4274
www.Xlibris.com
Orders@Xlibris.com

Baby Bird

One day a baby bird was born.
He was sleeping in an egg so warm.

He couldn't see the sun or moon,
although a little light would shine right through.

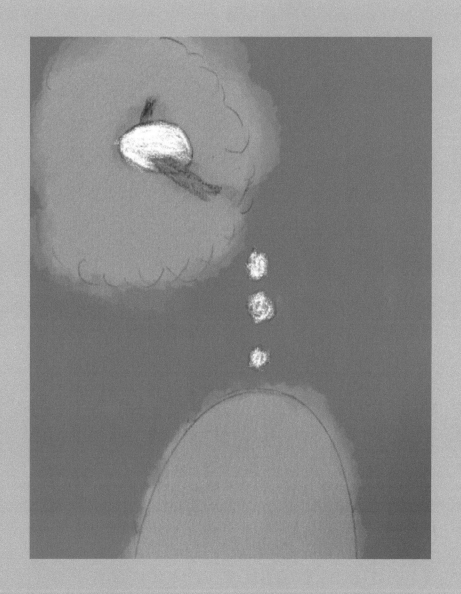

He couldn't fly or chirp or walk upon
the grass so sweet and soft.

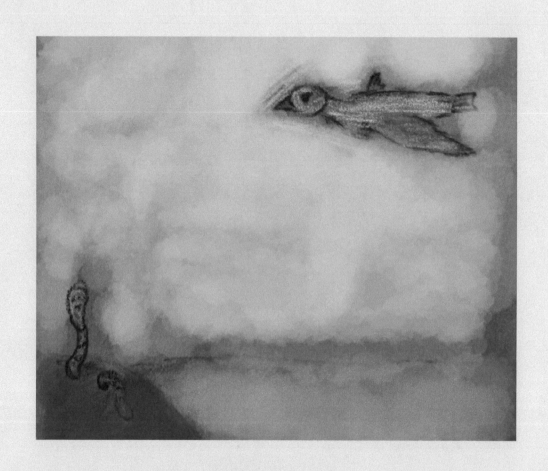

He hadn't tasted wiggly worms,

Or splashed in the bird bath in the morn.

Mother bird sat upon the egg to
keep it safe and warm.
She sat and sat and sat and sat, all
day long and through the night.

The sun came up and went back down.

Then the moon would do its round.

Days and nights went right on by.

Until one day the egg bounced about, it bounced
then wiggled with a peck, peck, peck.
With a crack and a chirp the egg opened up.

Out came baby bird to see the world.

Baby bird felt the bright warm sun.

He could see the moon in the darkest sky.

Finally, Baby bird had grown, with an eager hop he jumped to the ground.

He felt the soft sweet grass below.

He learned to dig for worms and eat them up.

He chirped a song in the morning light,

and splashed and splashed in the old bird bath.

Best of all baby bird spread his wings and he could fly!

CPSIA information can be obtained
at www.ICGtesting.com
Printed in the USA
BVHW021002270619
552118BV00003B/28/P